Dylan
The Villain
By K. G. CAMPBELL
PURPLE
VIKING

For Auntie Mairi and Uncle Roger,
who knew me when.

VIKING
An imprint of Penguin Random House LLC
375 Hudson Street
New York, New York 10014

First published in the United States of America by Viking, an imprint of Penguin Random House LLC, 2016

LIBRARY OF CONGRESS CATALOGING-IN-PUBLICATION DATA IS AVAILABLE.
ISBN: 978-0-451-47642-5

Manufactured in China

1 3 5 7 9 10 8 6 4 2

Book design by Jim Hoover   Set in Arno Pro and Giant Sized Spectacular
The artwork for this book was rendered in watercolor and colored pencil on tea-stained watercolor paper.

Mr. and Mrs. Snivels were minding their own business, when they happened to have a baby.

"Congratulations," said the doctor.
"It's a healthy little super-villain!"

Mrs. Snivels was quite surprised.

"There aren't any villains in the family," she said. "Or are there?"

Mr. Snivels didn't say anything (but there totally were).

The new parents named their little boy Dylan. They discovered that super-villain babies are much like any others.

They don’t like bedtime.

They throw their food.

They can even be allergic to everyday stuff . . .
like purple parsnip preserves.

But by and large, Dylan's parents figured
he was just about the best thing ever.

"Dylan's super-villain costume," they said, "is super scary.

"Dylan's super-villain laugh," they insisted, "is super crazy.

"Dylan's super-villain inventions," they boasted, "are extra-super villainous.

"You," they told Dylan, "are the very best and cleverest super-villain in the whole wide world!"

And Dylan totally agreed.

Until he went to school.

ASTRID RANCID'S
ACADEMY
FOR THE VILLAINOUS & VILE

Sure, Dylan's costume was scary.

But Addison Van Malice's was *bone-chilling*.

She has blue hair!
Who has *blue* hair?
Liam McLightning
Addison Van Malice

And yes, Dylan's laugh was crazy.
But Addison Van Malice's was *bananas*.

And Dylan's inventions were
certainly super villainous.
But Addison Van Malice's
were *demonic*!

"Honestly," grumbled Dylan. "The way people act around here, you'd think that I'm *not* the very best and cleverest super-villain in the whole wide world!"

He vowed to prove that he was.

His chance came one day when
Miss Slither announced a contest.

"This hideous trophy," she declared, "will be awarded to the pupil who creates the most diabolical robot. Principal Sinister will be the judge."

Each pupil was given a box of parts from the diabolical robot supply closet.

“That hideous trophy,” vowed Dylan, “will be mine! All MINE!”

Dylan worked feverishly
late into the night.

He sawed and he hammered.

He screwed and he glued.

He painted and he polished.

By midnight, Dylan had built a robot.

In the morning, Dylan gave his parents a demonstration.

"Look," he said.
"It has telescopic arms.

"It has monster claws.

"It even has an astro-plasm cannon."

“That,” said Mr. and Mrs. Snivels, “is the very best, most diabolical robot in the whole wide world.”
And Dylan totally agreed.

Until he went to school.

Sure, Dylan's robot was diabolical.
In fact it was more diabolical than anyone else's.

Except one.

“Look!” said Addison Van Malice.
“It has titanium armor . . .
and evil laser eyes.

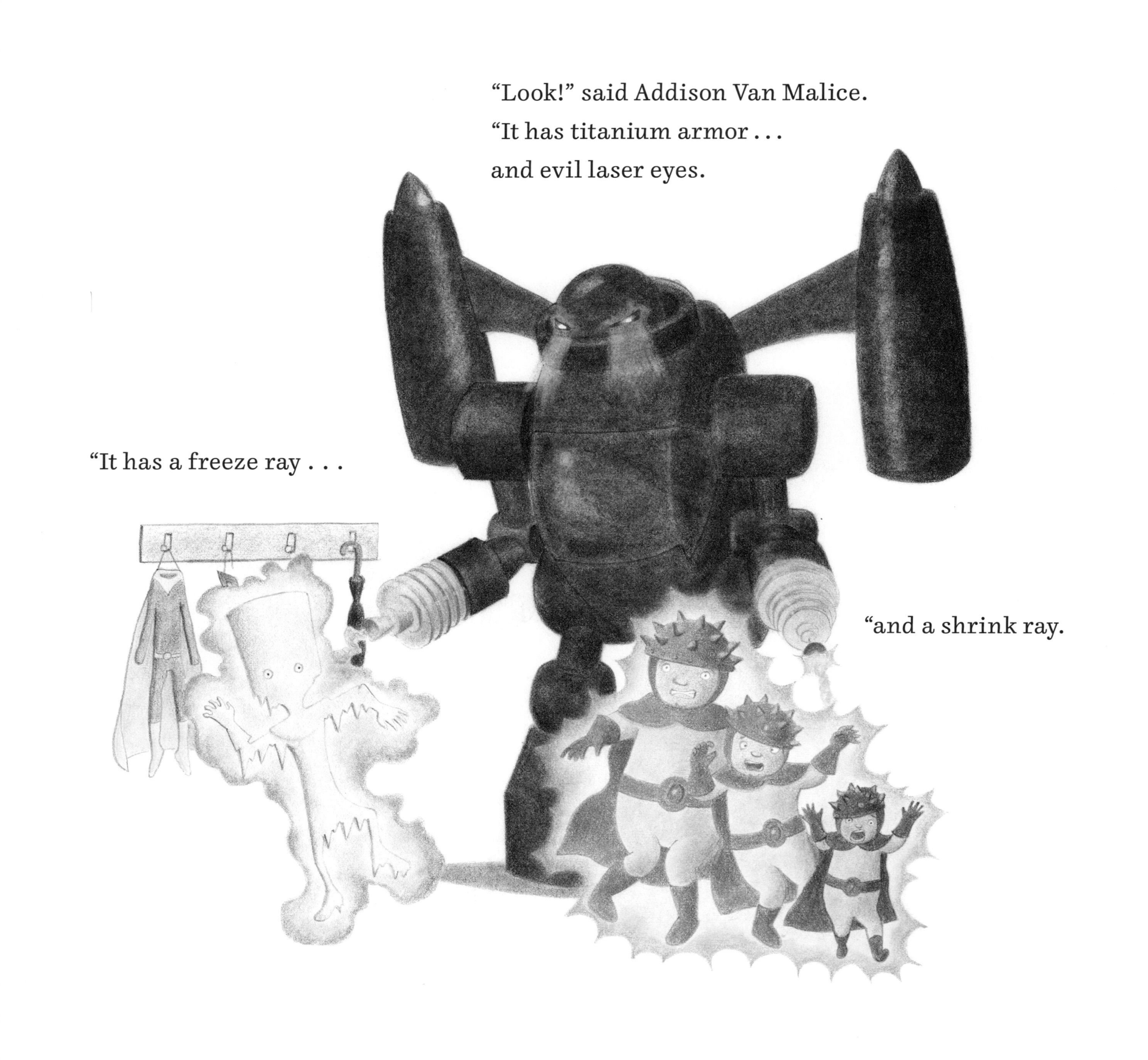

“It has a freeze ray . . .

“and a shrink ray.

"It even has a cockpit,
and supersonic rockets
for space travel."

"What does this do?" said Dylan.

When Principal Sinister arrived, Dylan's
robot was the most diabolical in the class.
"Where is Addison Van Malice?" said the principal.
"We don't know," said everyone.

And that was quite true.

Dylan won the hideous trophy.

It was a little sticky . . .

. . . but Dylan didn't care.

He cuddled it all night.

Unfortunately, the sticky, hideous trophy gave Dylan an allergic reaction. It was almost like someone had put purple parsnip preserves on it.

On *purpose*.

“That,” said Mr. and Mrs. Snivels, “is the very ugliest, most uncomfortable-looking allergic reaction in the whole wide world.”

And Dylan totally agreed.

...THE END?

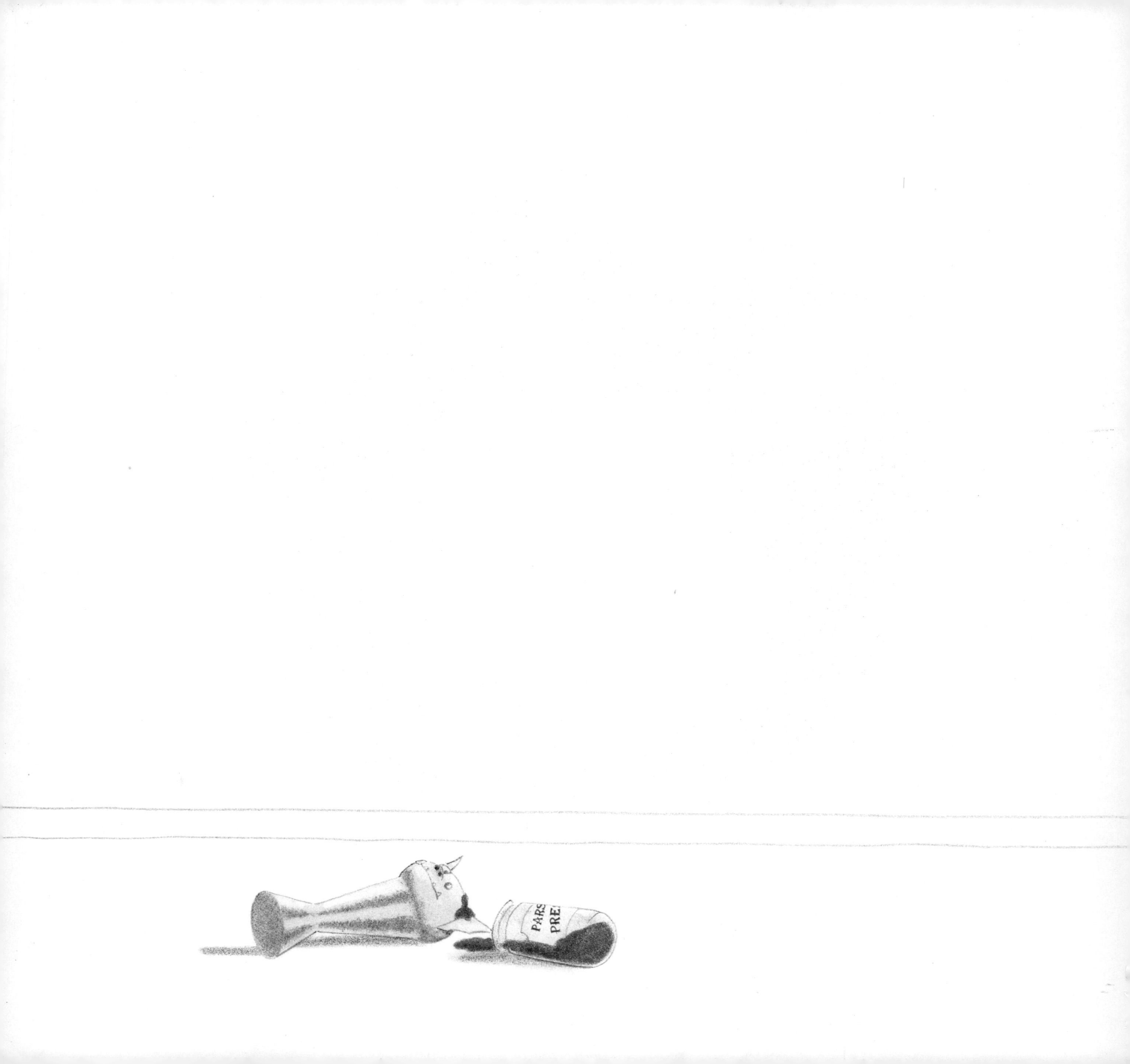